RAD!

WRITTEN BY
ANNE BUSTARD

ILLUSTRATED BY
DANIEL WISEMAN

ABRAMS BOOKS FOR YOUNG READERS • NEW YORK

To Ella, Theo, Grace, and Katie
—AB

To the two RADDEST dudes I know,
Henry and Hugo!
—DW

The illustrations in this book were created digitally with Photoshop,
using custom brushes and textures.

Library of Congress Control Number 2019942481

ISBN 978-1-4197-4101-2

Text copyright © 2020 Anne S. Bustard
Illustration copyright © 2020 Daniel Wiseman
Book design by Steph Stilwell

Printed and bound in China
10 9 8 7 6 5 4 3 2 1

Abrams Books for Young Readers are available at
special discounts when purchased in quantity for premiums
and promotions as well as fundraising or educational use.
Special editions can also be created to specification. For details,
contact specialsales@abramsbooks.com or the address below.

Abrams® is a registered trademark of Harry N. Abrams, Inc.

ABRAMS The Art of Books
195 Broadway, New York, NY 10007
abramsbooks.com

ESTHER

CHESTER

LESTER

HESTER

SYLVESTER

Skate! says Esther.

Stoked? says Chester.

Totally! say Hester and Sylvester.

Never, says Lester.

Never? says Esther.
Never? says Chester.
Why? say Hester and Sylvester.

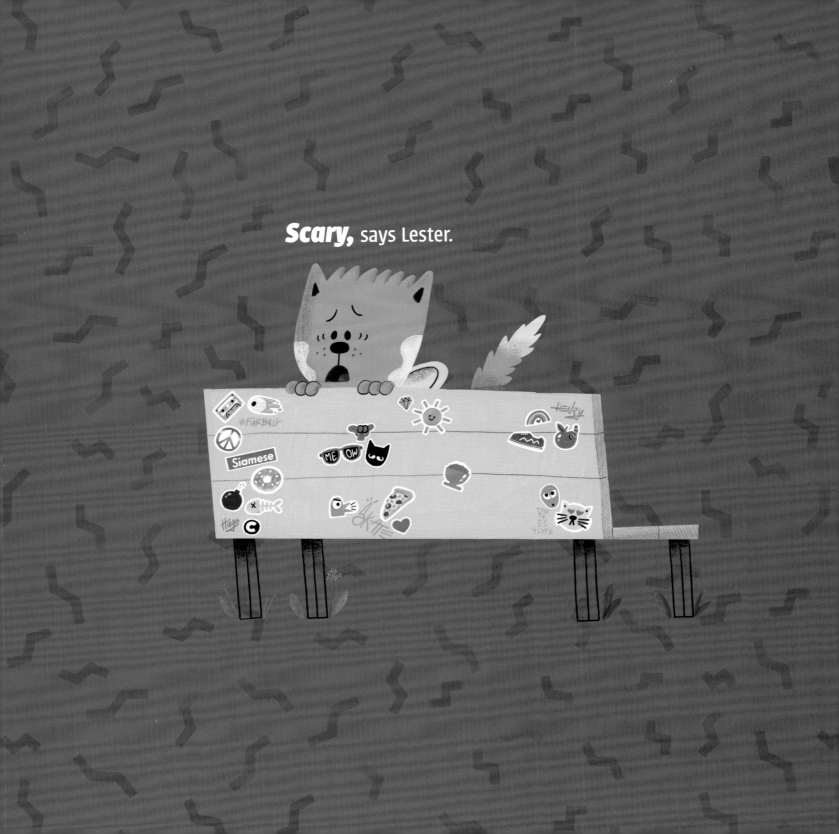

Practice, says Esther.
C'mon! says Chester.
Yeah! say Hester and Sylvester.

Nope, says Lester.

Try, says Esther.
Please? says Chester.

Start! say Hester and Sylvester.
No, says Lester.

No? says Esther.
No? says Chester.
Roll! say Hester and Sylvester.

RAD! says Esther.

RAD! says Chester.

RAD! say Hester and Sylvester.

Maybe, says Lester.

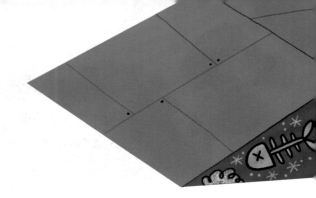

Awesome! says Esther.

Gnarly! says Chester.

Cool! say Hester and Sylvester.

Ready, says Lester.

Go! says Esther.

Steady? says Chester.

Alright! say Hester and Sylvester.

Wipeout! says Lester.

Again, says Esther.

Now! says Chester.
Yesss! say Hester and Sylvester.

Almost, says Esther.

Close!
says Chester.

Better!
say Hester and Sylvester.

RAD!

says Lester.

Sweet! says Esther.
Righteous! says Chester.
Woot! say Hester and Sylvester.

Tomorrow! says Lester.

No, no, no, no way!
say Esther, Chester, Hester, and Sylvester.